NORMAN BRIDWELL

Clifford's
ABC

scarecrow

elephant

dog

elf

ISBN 0-590-44286-4

45 44 43 42   7 8 9/0

Printed in the U.S.A.   23

NORMAN BRIDWELL
Clifford's
ABC

alligator

beaver

cow

SCHOLASTIC INC.
New York   Toronto   London   Auckland   Sydney

A a

accordion

axe

armadillo

anvil

acorns

ant

anchor

alligator

Bb

bird

ball

bat

boots

basket

balloon

boy

boat

butterfly

beaver

bottle

baby

Cc

collar

cow

cat

cook

candle

cake

cactus

cape

clown

checks

Dd

dragon

dolphin

dog

dummy

drum

derby

dandelion

Ee
eagle
earring
eel
egg
elephant
elf
Eskimo

eagle

egg

E e

earring

elephant

elf

eel

Eskimo

Ff

flag

frog

fly

fish

fire

fairy

flea

funnel

flower

fox

ghost

gorilla

giraffe

Gg

garden

goat

Gg
garbage can
garden
ghost
giraffe
glove
goat
gorilla

glove

garbage can

Hh

helicopter

harp

house

horse

hollyhock

hummingbird

hat

horn

haystack

hippopotamus

Ii

iguana

ice cream cone

igloo

iris

ink

iron

Jj

jet

juggler

jogger

jack-o'-lantern

jester

jacks

Kk   Ll

koala

lobster

lily

lasso

knight

lumberjack

karate

knitting

log

kitten

kangaroo

leopard

lamb

lion

kayak

Mm

moon

mop

map

mask

monkey

mittens

mouse

magician

marionette

magnet

Nn

nest
net
noodles
note
nun
nurse
nut
nutcracker

Oo

owl

orchid

ostrich

octopus

orange

overalls

oar

P

P p

parachute

palm

pineapple

panda

picture

pirate

paintbrush

pear

palette

pony

pig

porcupine

Qq

quail

quartet

question

queen

quilt

Rr
rabbit
raccoon
racket
radishes
rain
rainbow
rake
rhinoceros
robot
rocket
roller skate
rope
rug

Rr

rain

rhinoceros

rainbow

rocket

robot

rope

racket

rug

raccoon

rabbit

rake

roller skate

radishes

Ss

Saturn

star

scarecrow

sleep

saxophone

soccer ball

sausage

saxophone

seesaw

sandwich

seal

squirrel

snail

stool

Tt

tepee

tractor

tent

tiger

telescope

television

teapot

train

teddy bear

turtle

table

Uu

umbrella

UFO

unicorn

umpire

urn

ukulele

unicycle

V v

volcano

vampire

valentine

violets

violin

vise

vacuum cleaner

vase

Ww

whale

waves

walrus

wrenches

wheelbarrow

witch

wolf

worm

waffles

wagon

Xx Yy

xylophone

yacht

x-ray

yak

yawn

yarn

yo-yo

Xx
x-ray
xylophone

Yy
yacht
yak
yarn
yawn
yo-yo

zeppelin

Zz

Zz
zebra
zeppelin
zipper
zither
zoo

ZOO

zebra

zipper

zither

z